MARVEL

THE COURAGEOUS
CAPTAIN AMERICA

Adapted by Billy Wrecks
Based on the Marvel comic book series CAPTAIN AMERICA
Illustrated by Val Semeiks, Scott McLeod, The Storybook Art Group,
and Hi-Fi Colour Design

 A GOLDEN BOOK • NEW YORK

MARVEL, CAPTAIN AMERICA, and all related characters and the distinctive likeness thereof are trademarks of Marvel
Entertainment, LLC, and all its subsidiaries, and are used with permission. Copyright © 2011 Marvel Entertainment, LLC, and its
subsidiaries. Licensed by Marvel Characters B.V. www.marvel.com. All rights reserved. Published in the United States by Golden
Books, an imprint of Random House Children's Books, a division of Random House, Inc., 1745 Broadway, New York, NY 10019,
and in Canada by Random House of Canada Limited, Toronto. Golden Books, A Golden Book, A Little Golden Book,
the G colophon, and the distinctive gold spine are registered trademarks of Random House, Inc.
www.randomhouse.com/kids
Educators and librarians, for a variety of teaching tools, visit us at www.randomhouse.com/teachers
ISBN: 978-0-307-93050-7
Printed in the United States of America
10 9 8 7 6 5 4 3 2 1
Random House Children's Books supports the First Amendment and celebrates the right to read.

America has always been the land of opportunity. People come to America from all over the world for the freedom to make their dreams come true.

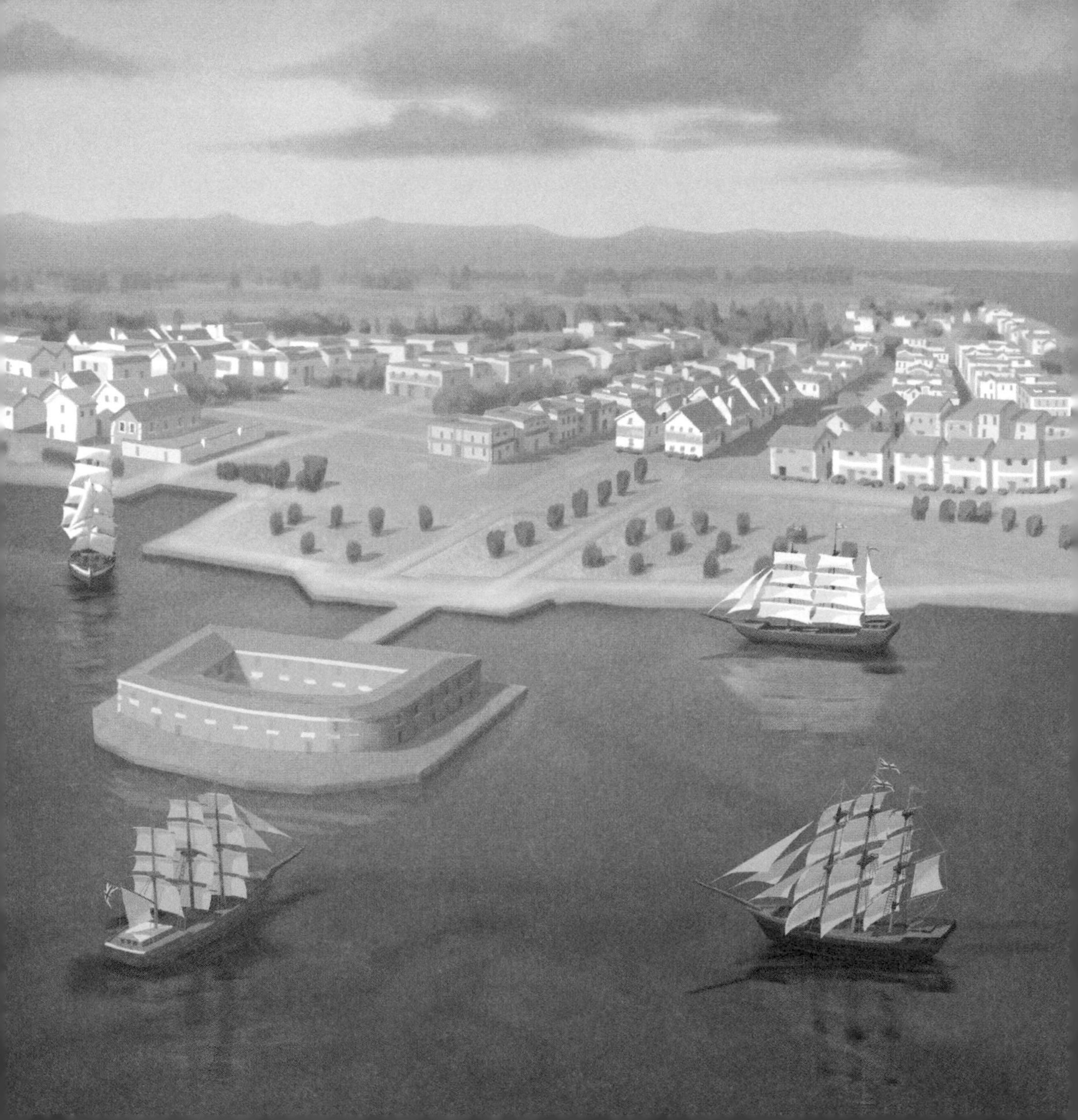

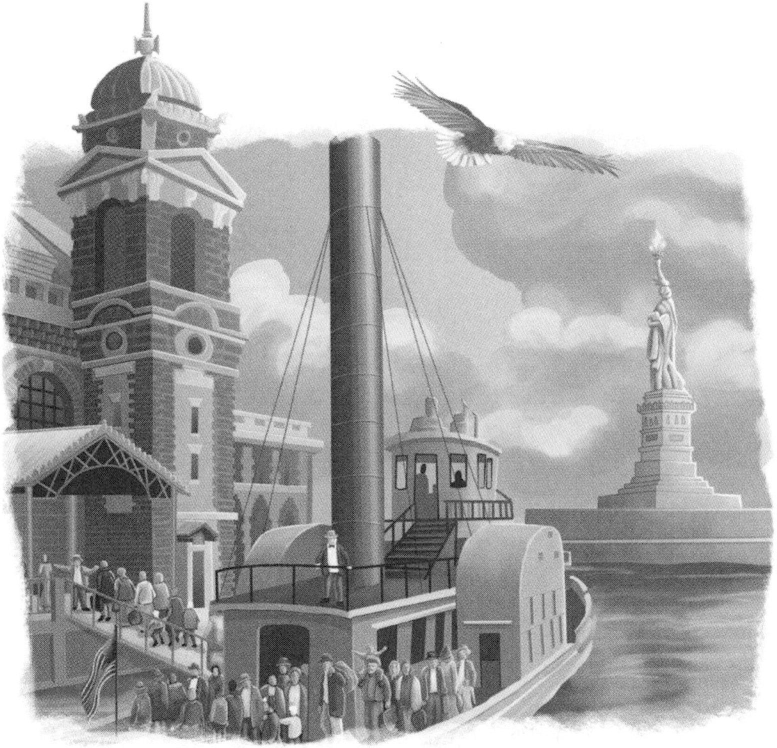

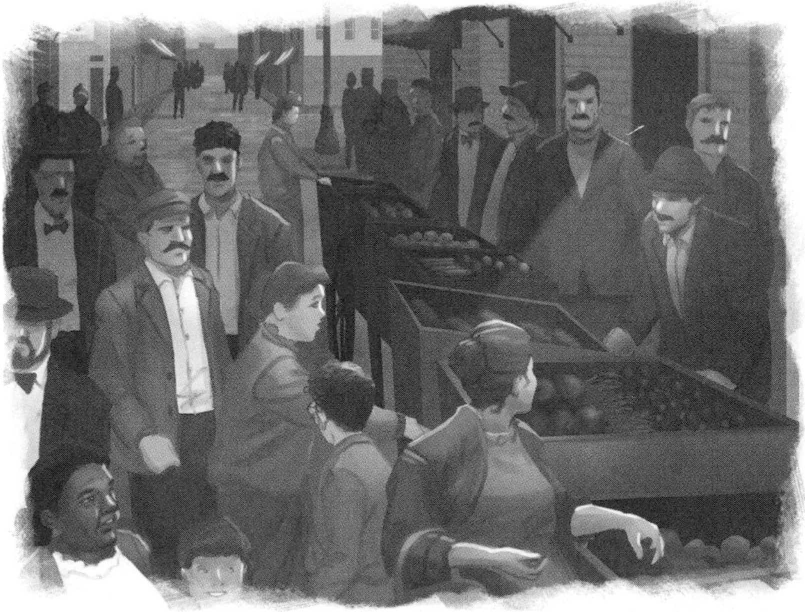

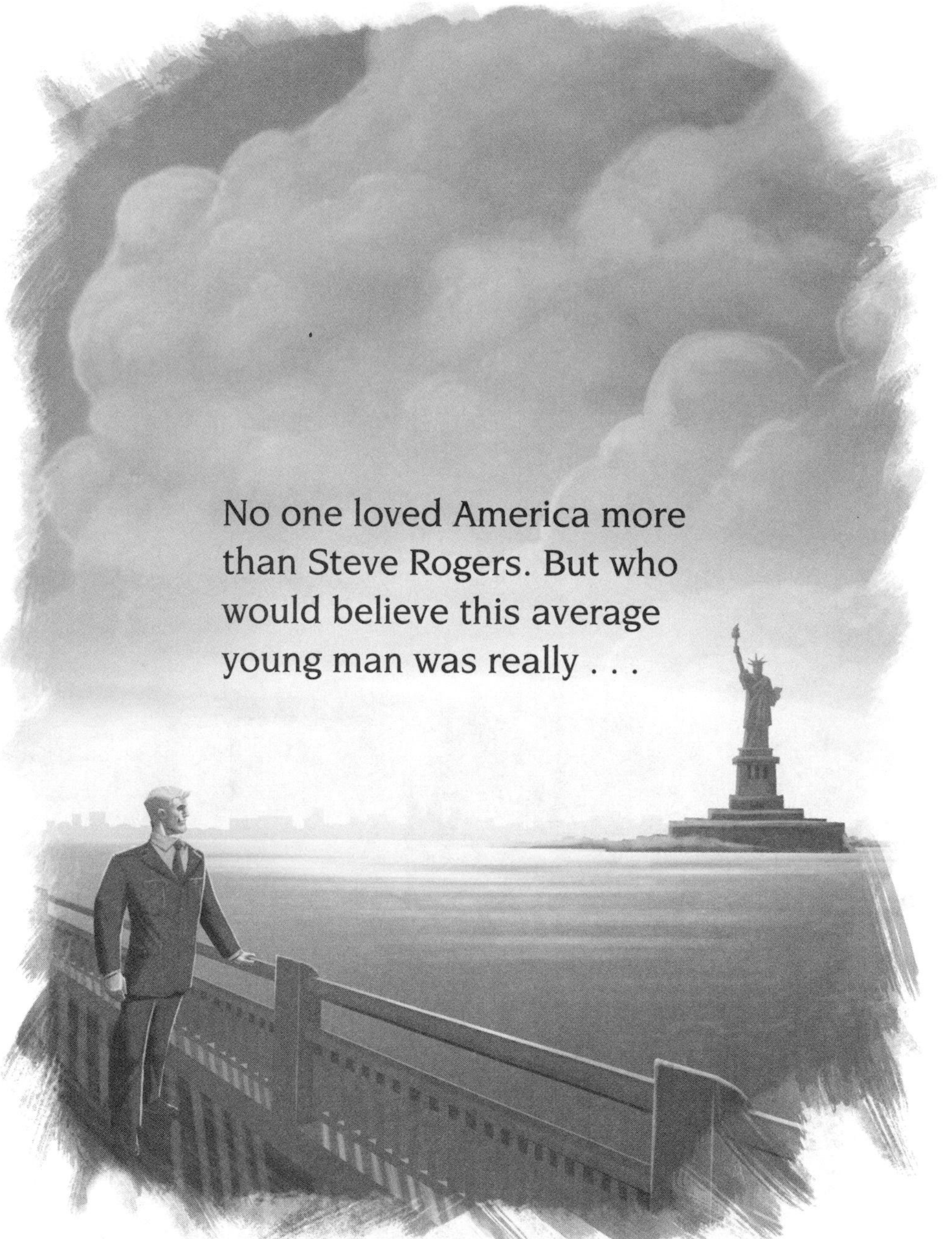

No one loved America more than Steve Rogers. But who would believe this average young man was really . . .

CAPTAIN AMERICA!

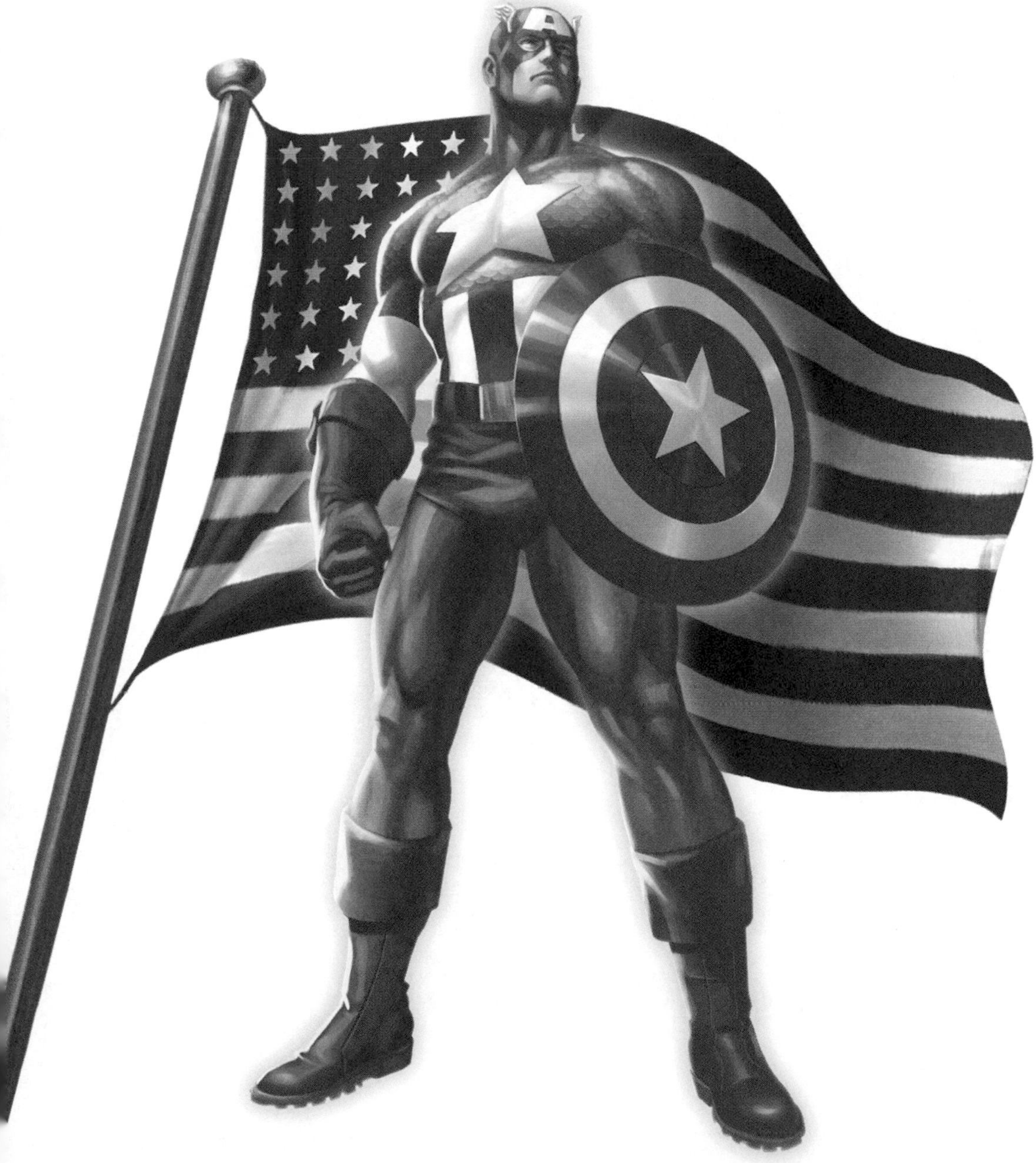

In times of trouble . . .

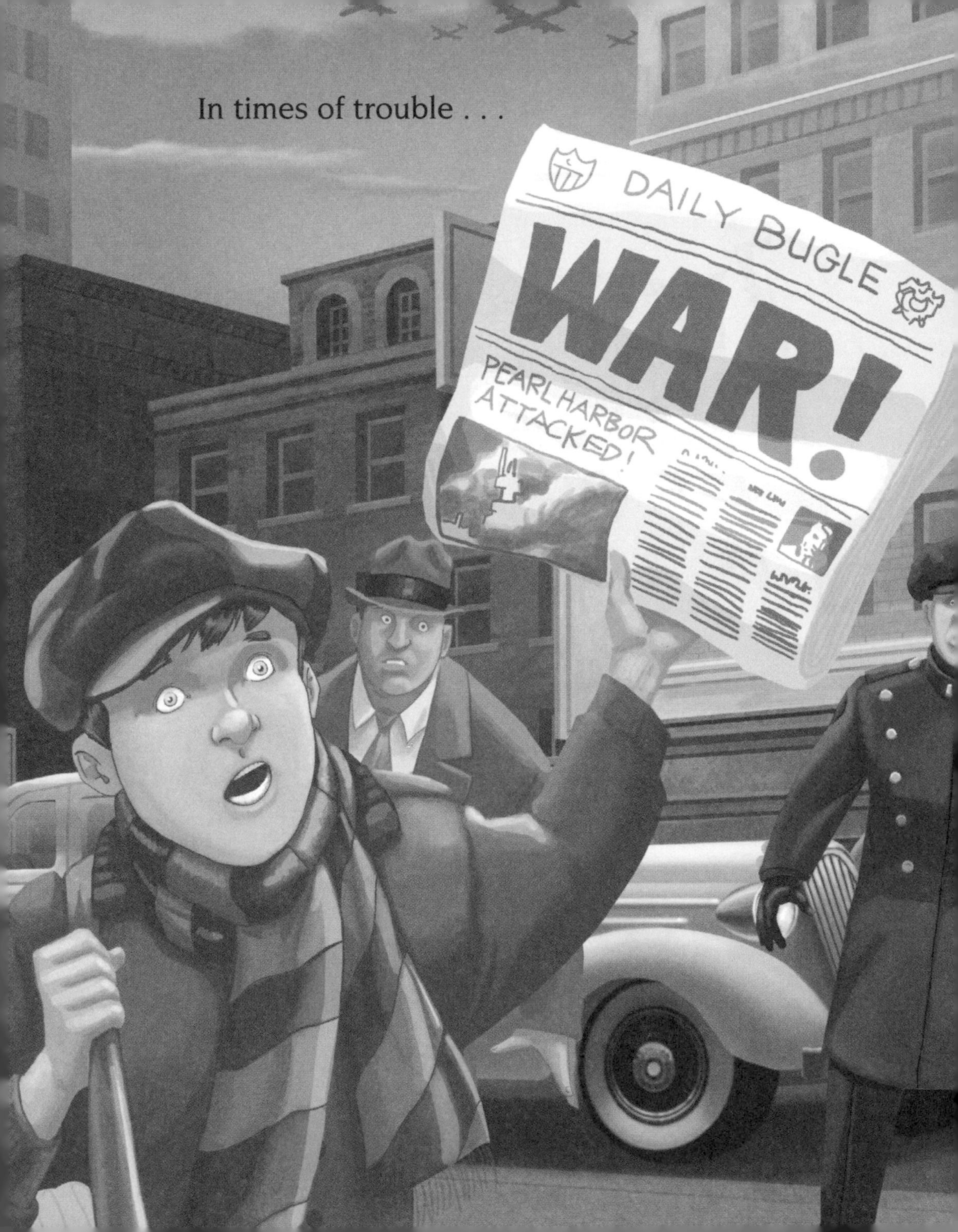
DAILY BUGLE
WAR!
PEARL HARBOR ATTACKED!

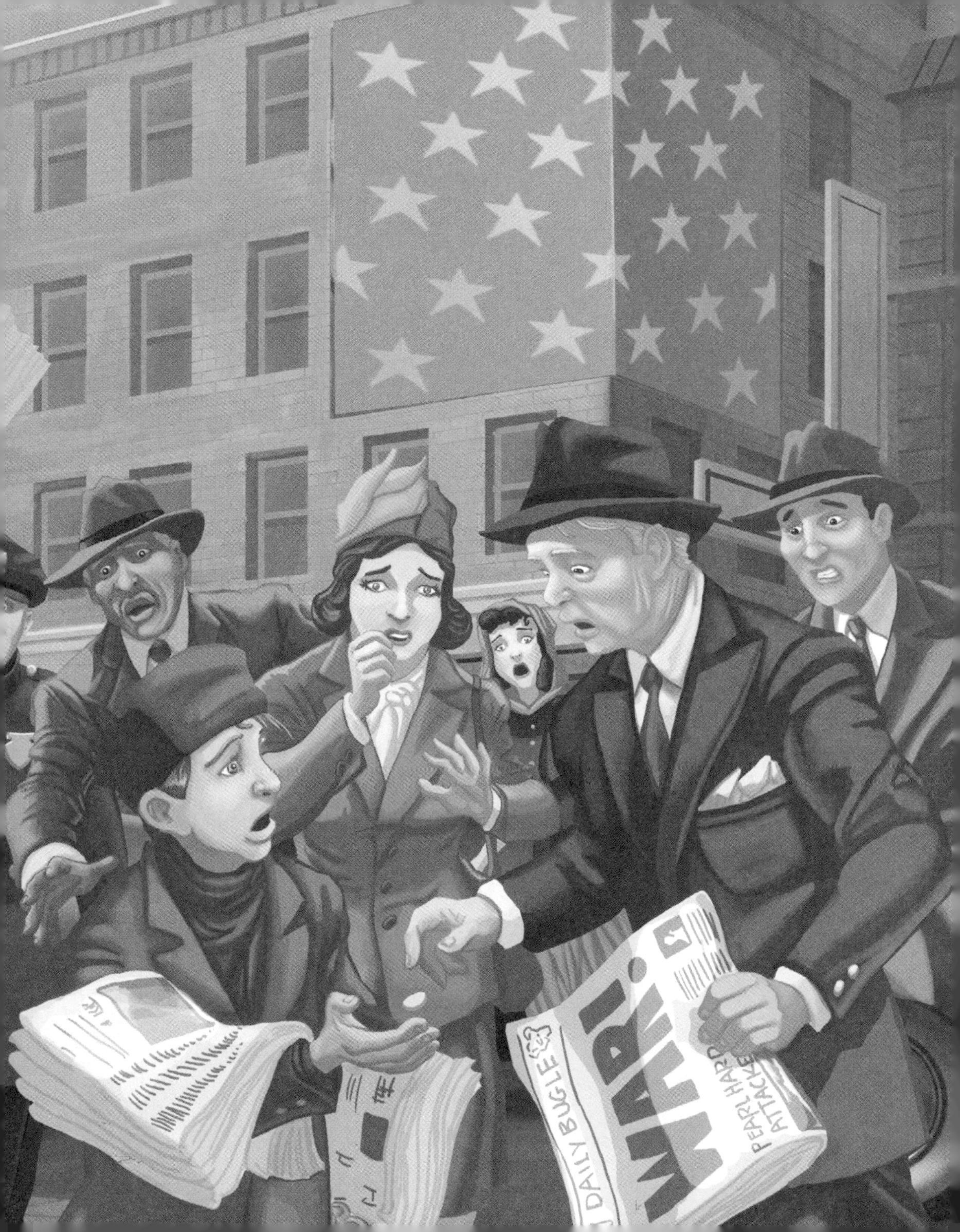
DAILY BUGLE
WAR!

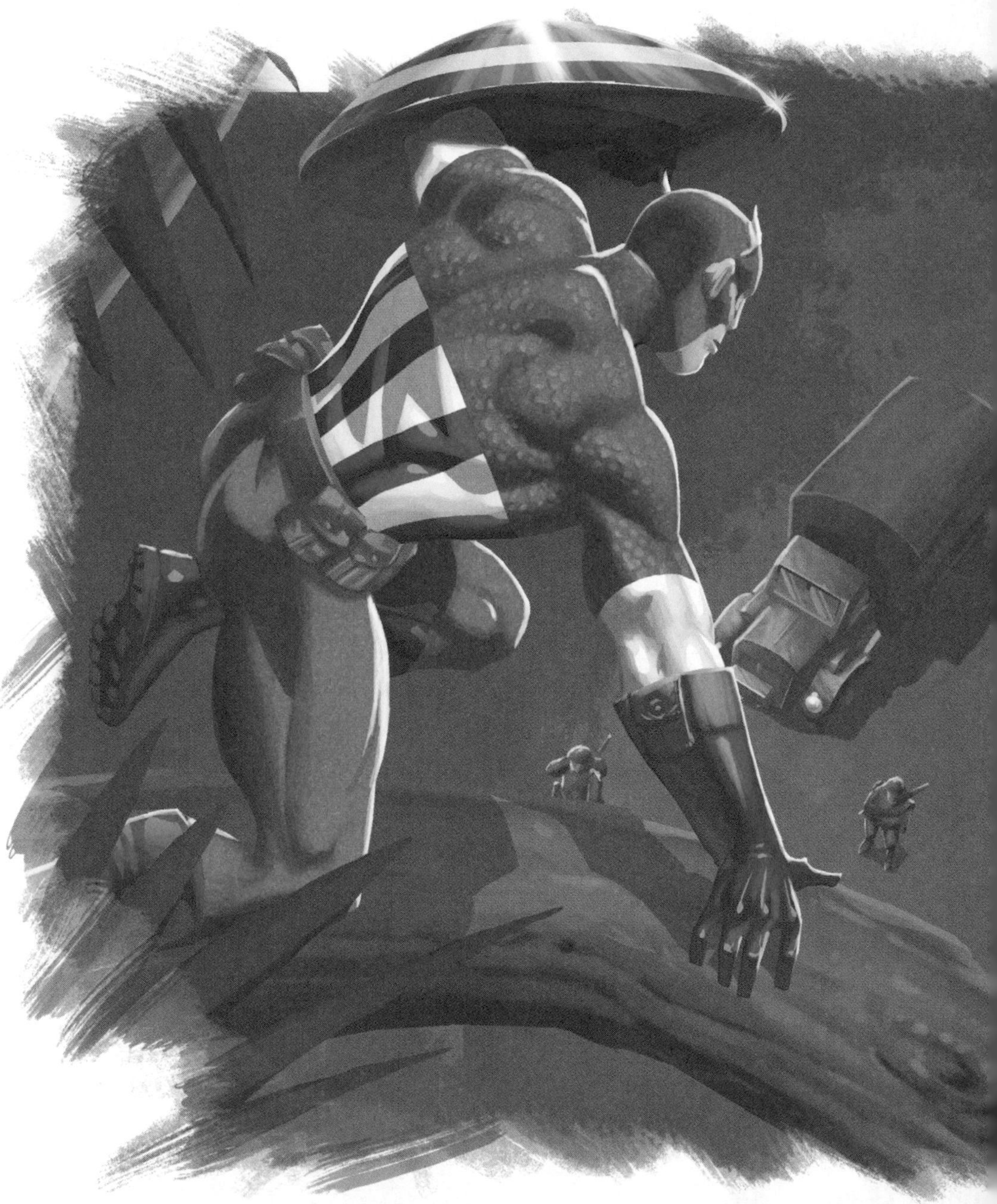

. . . Captain America was ready to face any **challenge**.

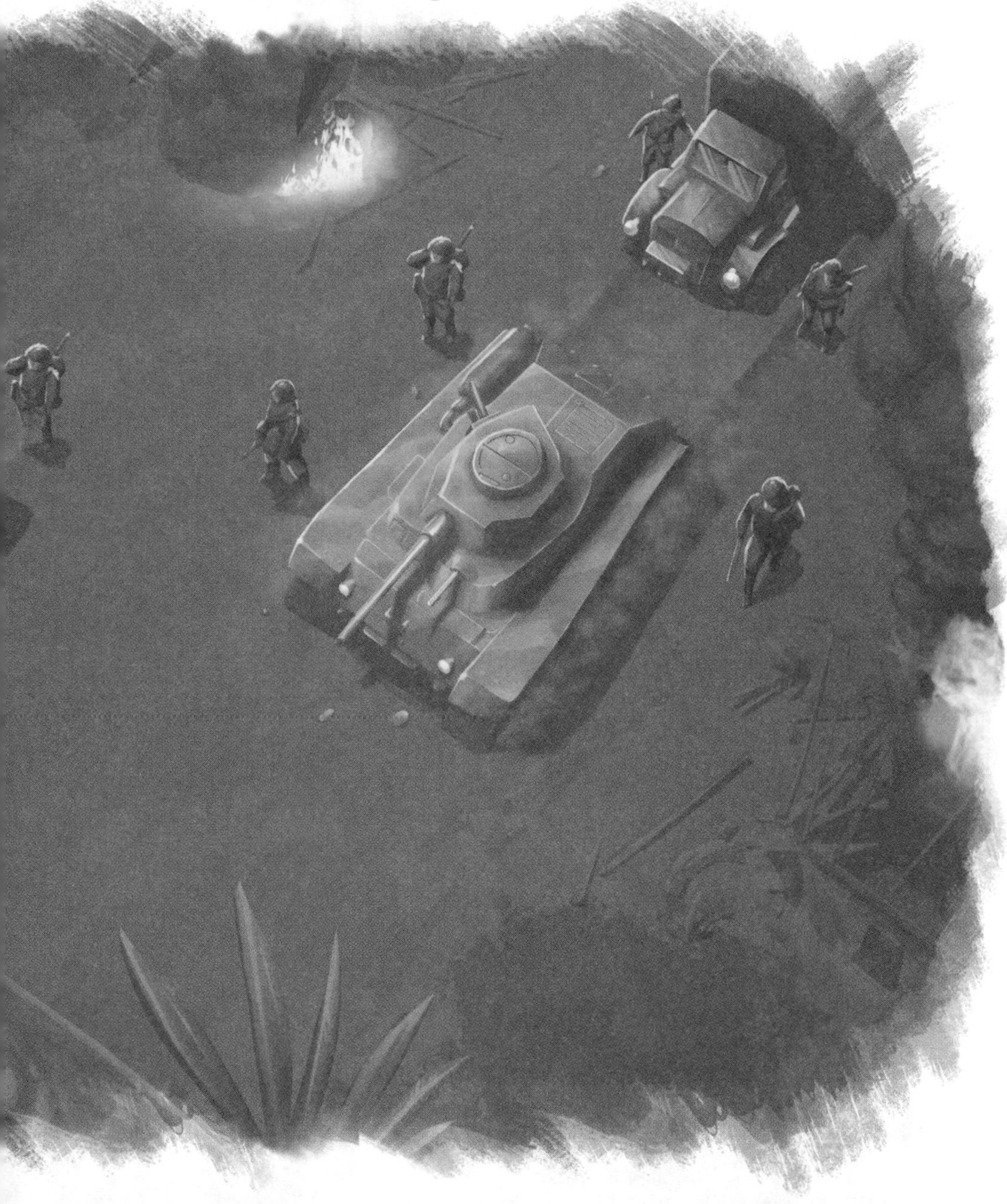

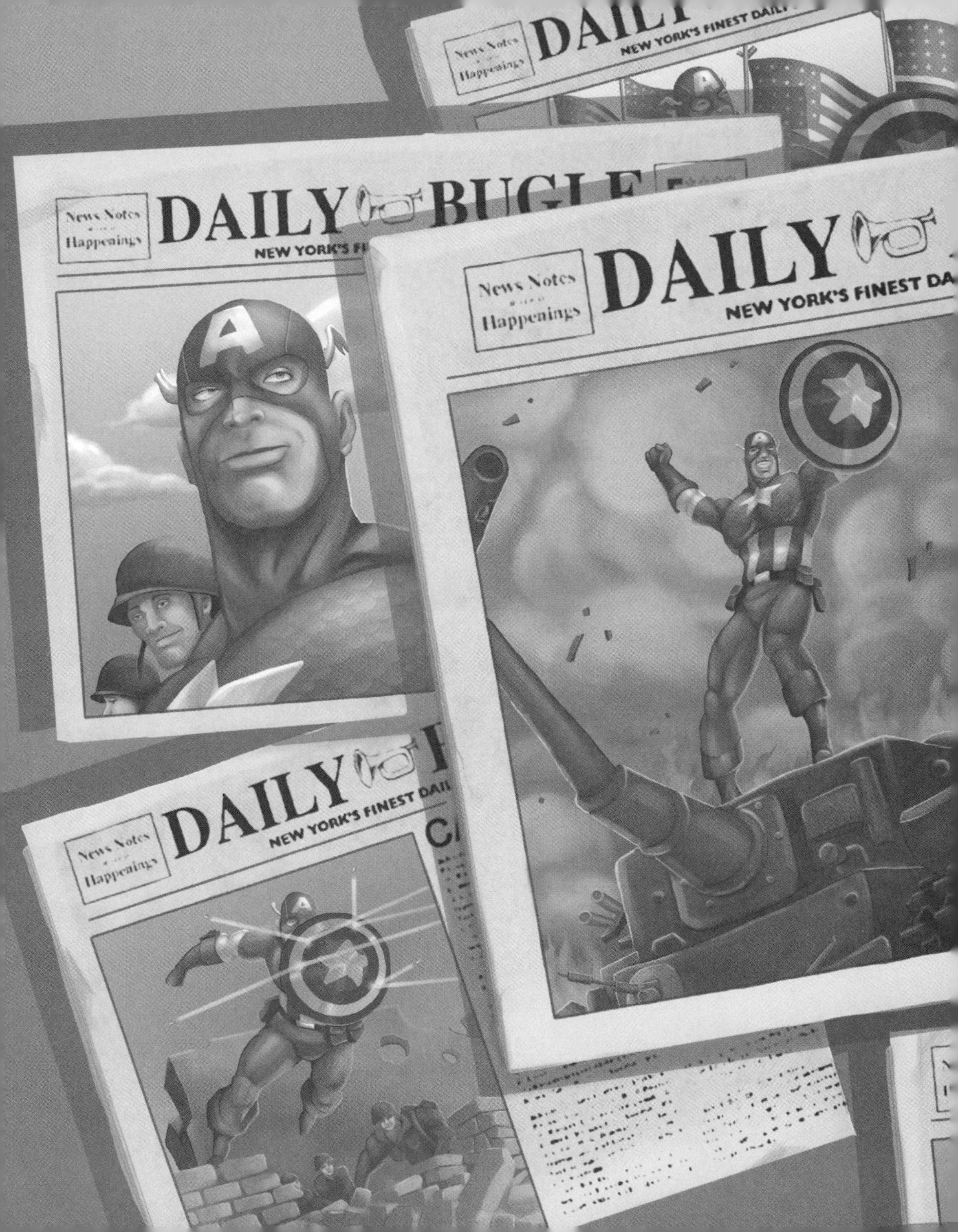

DAILY
NEW YORK'S FINEST DAILY
News Notes
Happenings
DAILY BUGLE
NEW YORK'S FI
News Notes
Happenings
DAILY
NEW YORK'S FINEST DA
News Notes
Happenings
DAILY
NEW YORK'S FINEST DAIL
News Notes
Happenings
CA

Captain America was a hero whose **amazing** deeds and adventures were known to everyone.

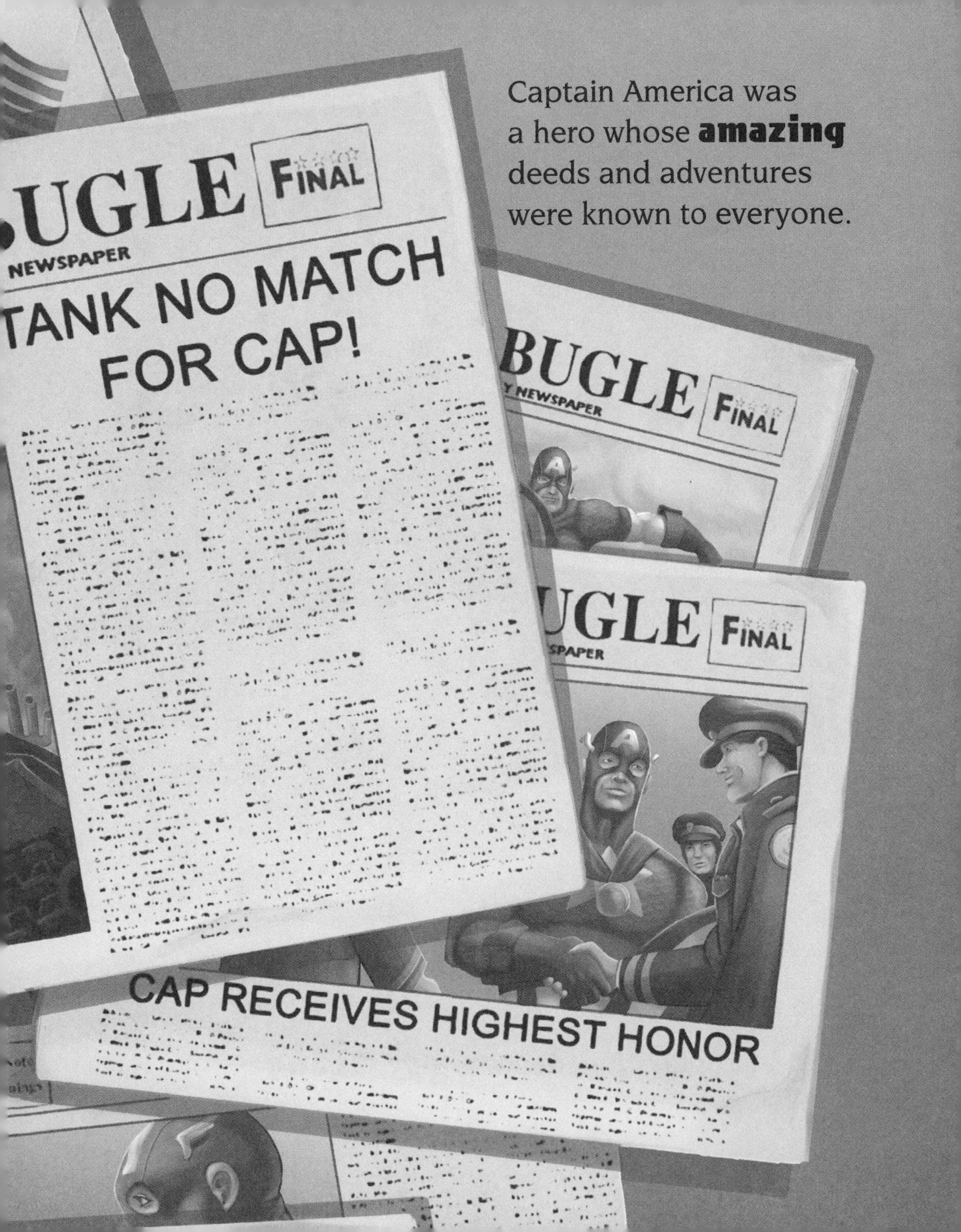
UGLE
FINAL
NEWSPAPER
TANK NO MATCH FOR CAP!
BUGLE
FINAL
NEWSPAPER
UGLE
FINAL
SPAPER
CAP RECEIVES HIGHEST HONOR

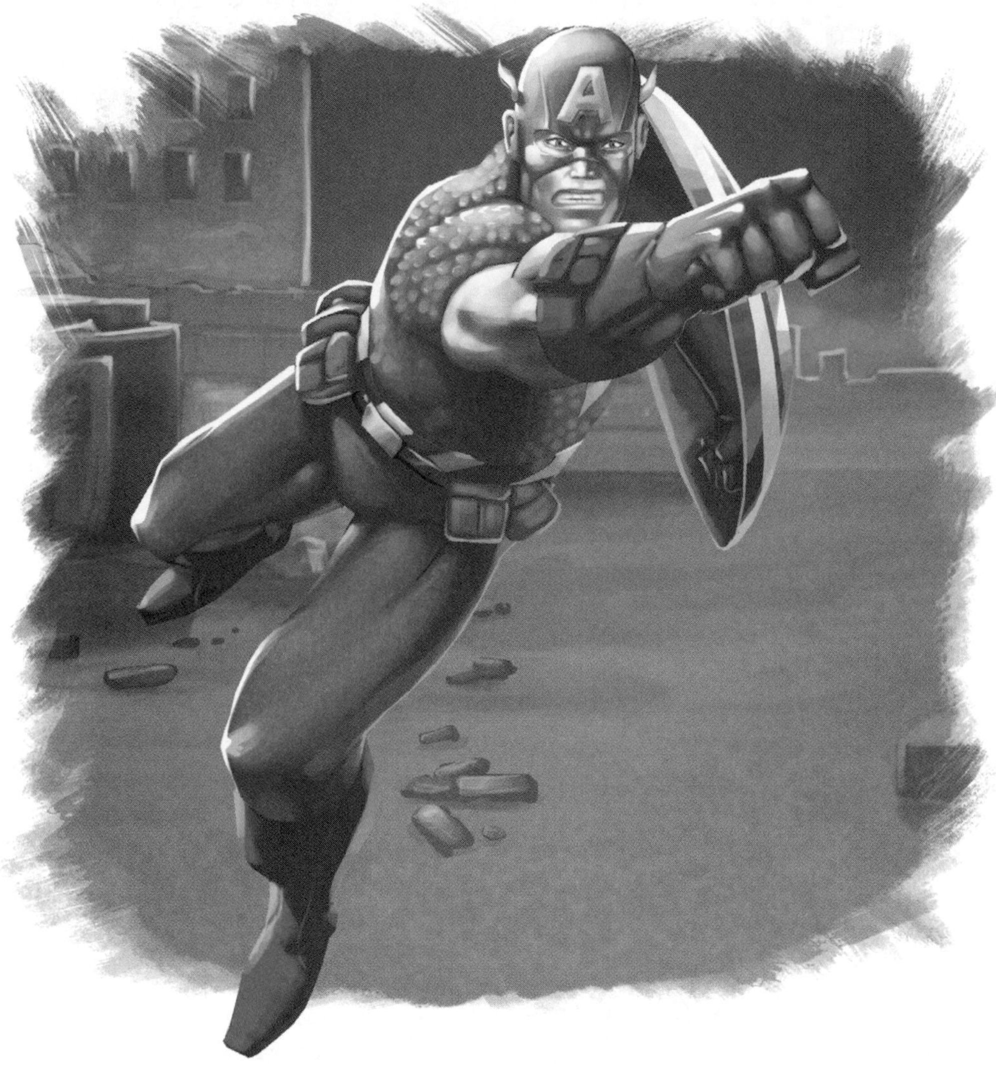

Captain America was very **strong** . . .

and he was very **fast**.

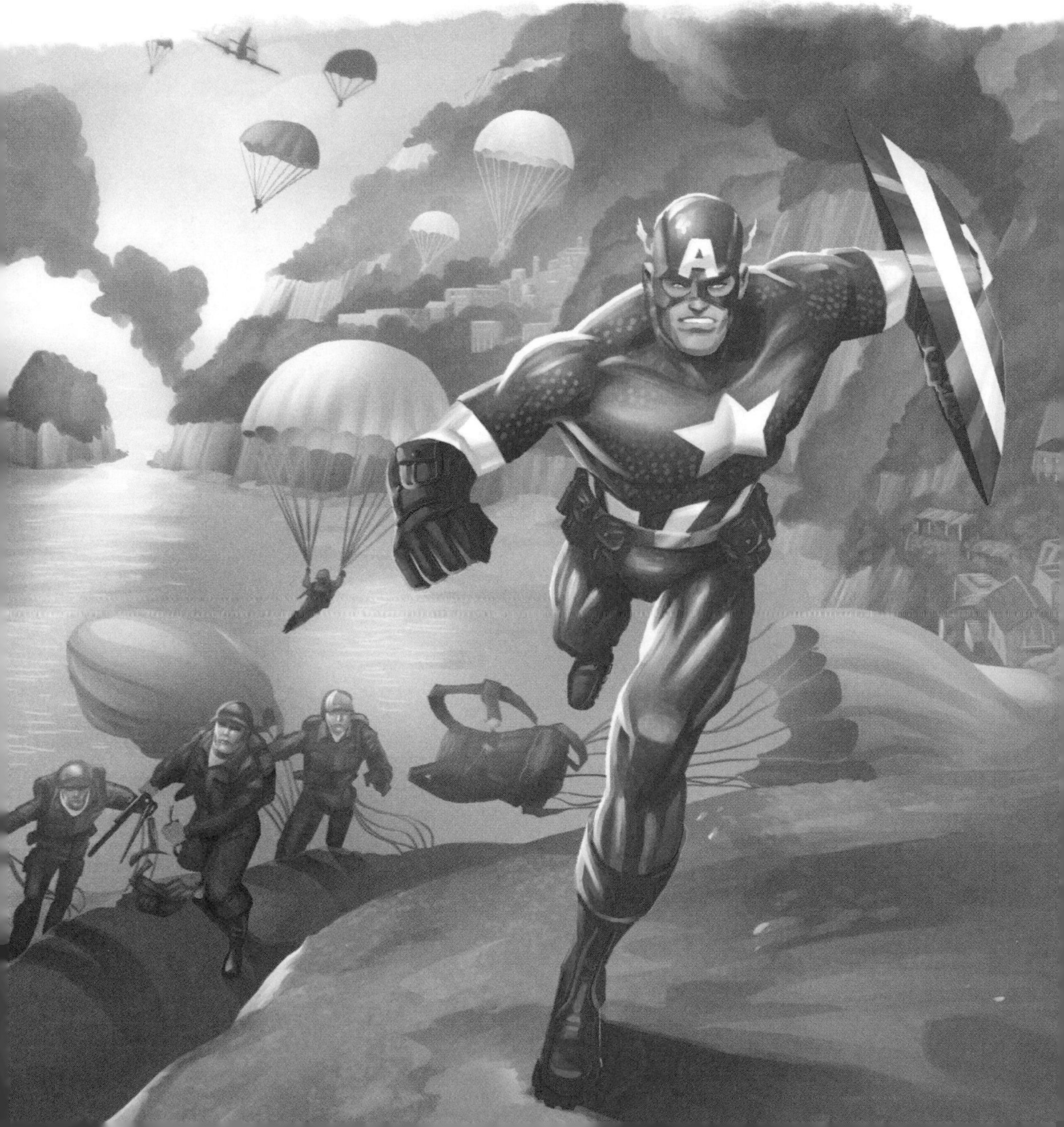

Captain America **bravely** traveled anywhere he was needed.

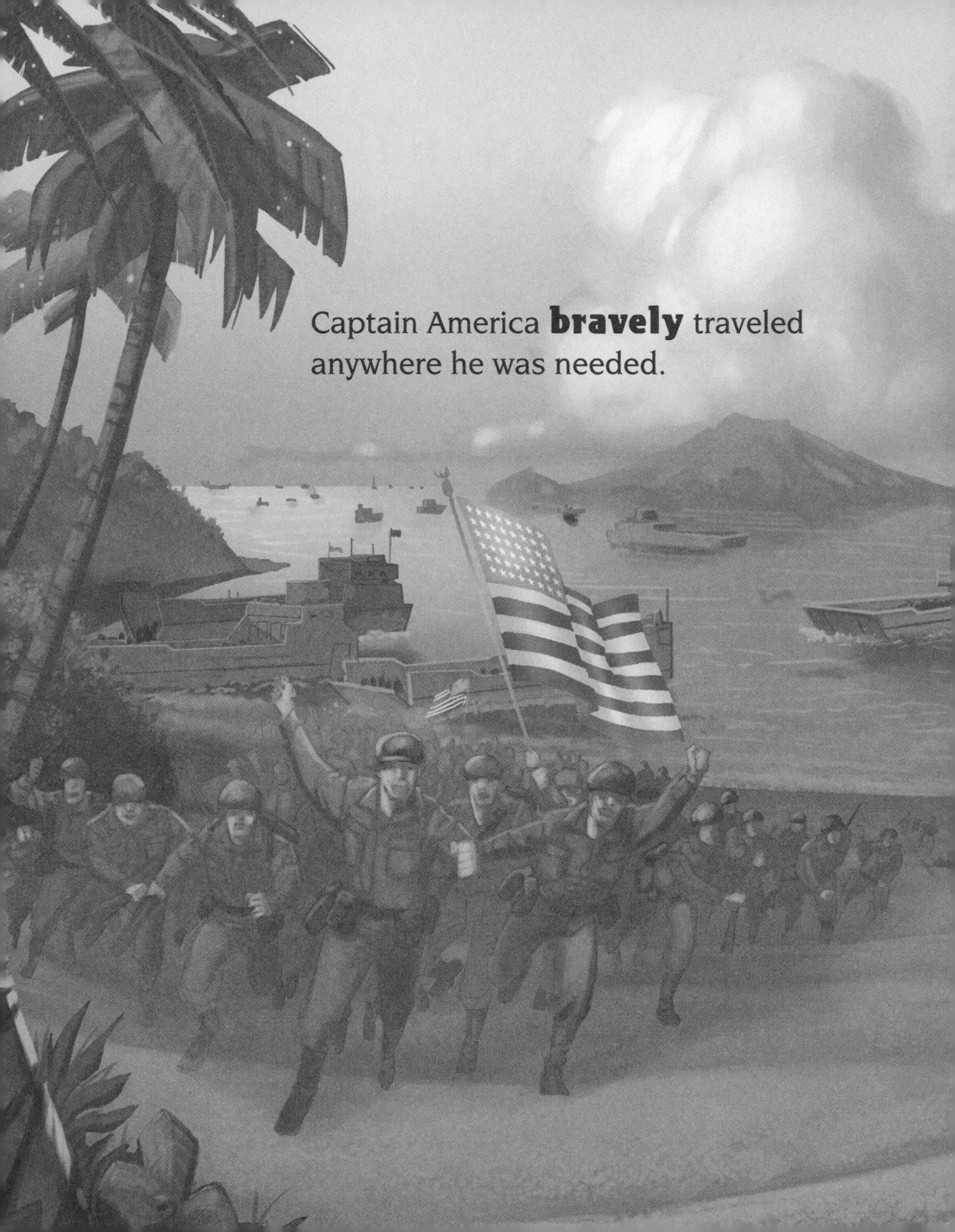

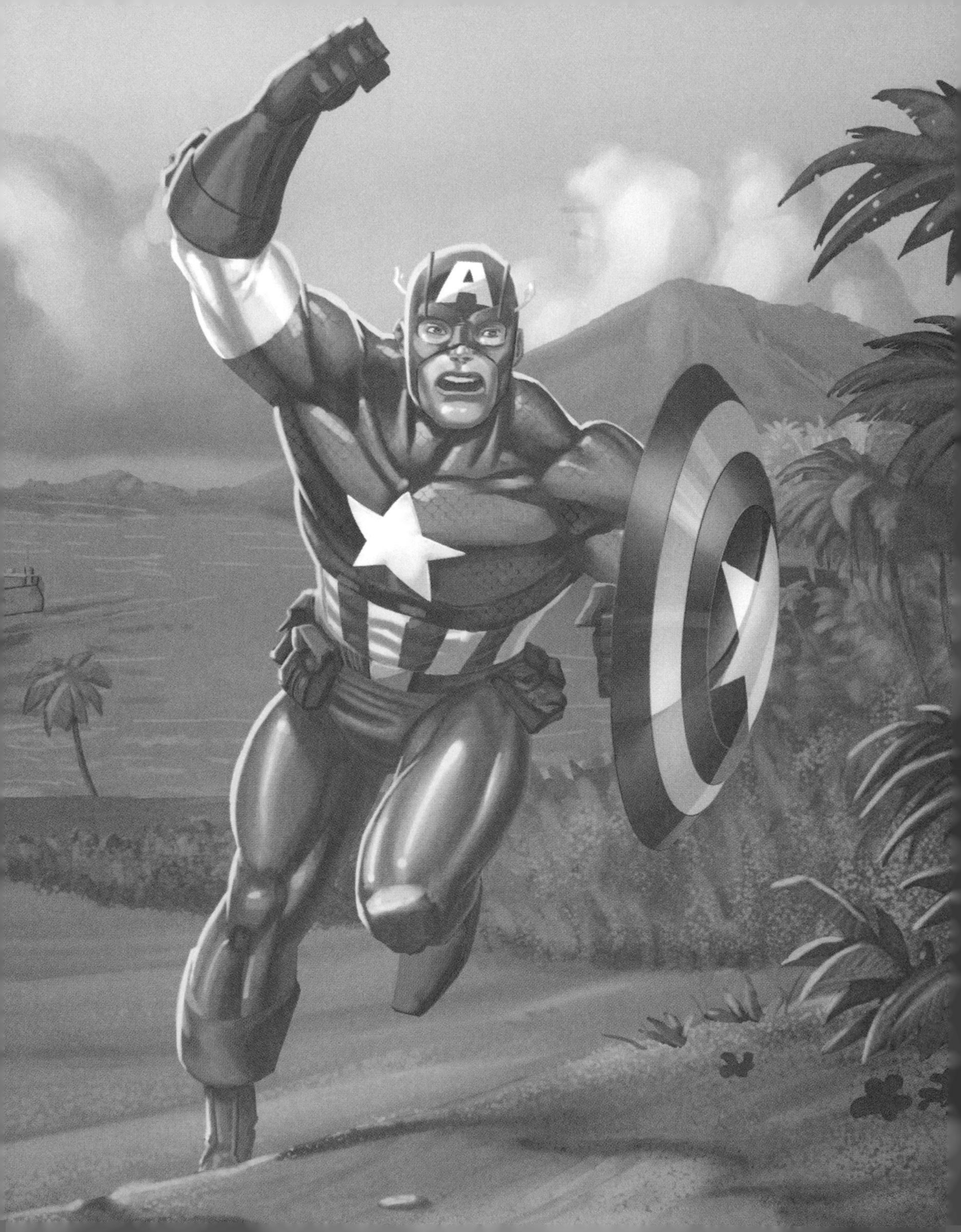

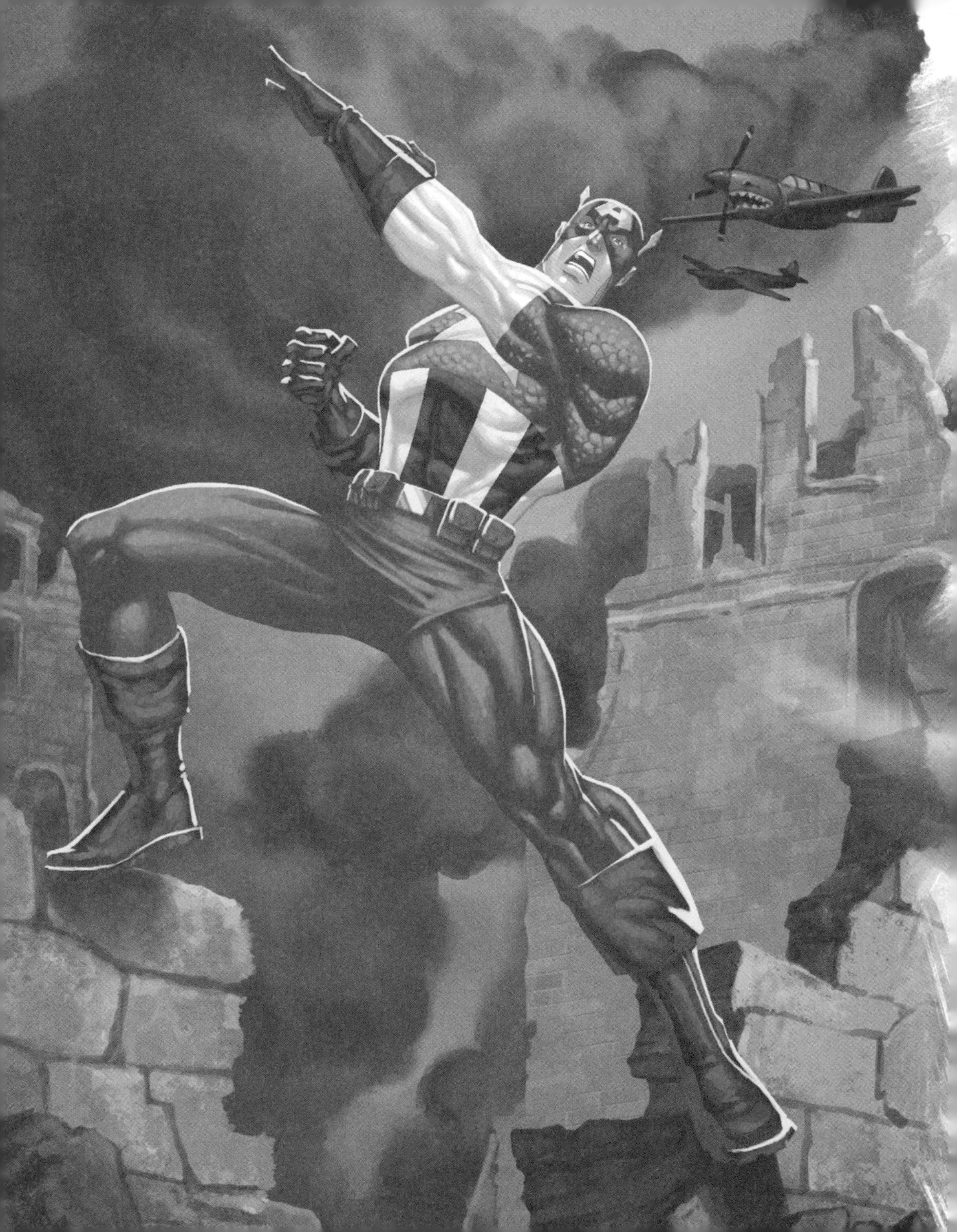

Captain America used an **unbreakable** shield that could knock over any foe.

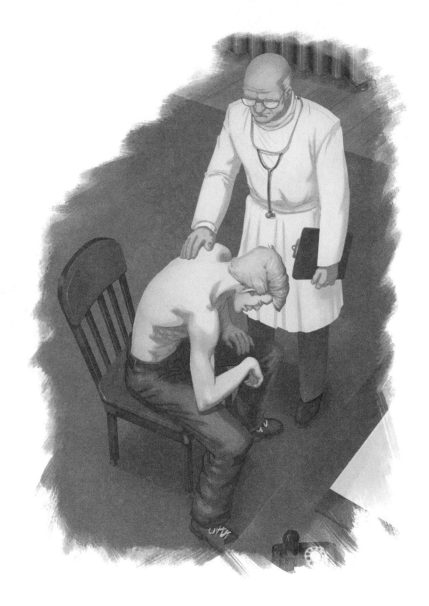

But Steve Rogers had not always been so fit.
In fact, he had once been weak and sickly.

So he agreed to be part of a **super-secret** experiment.

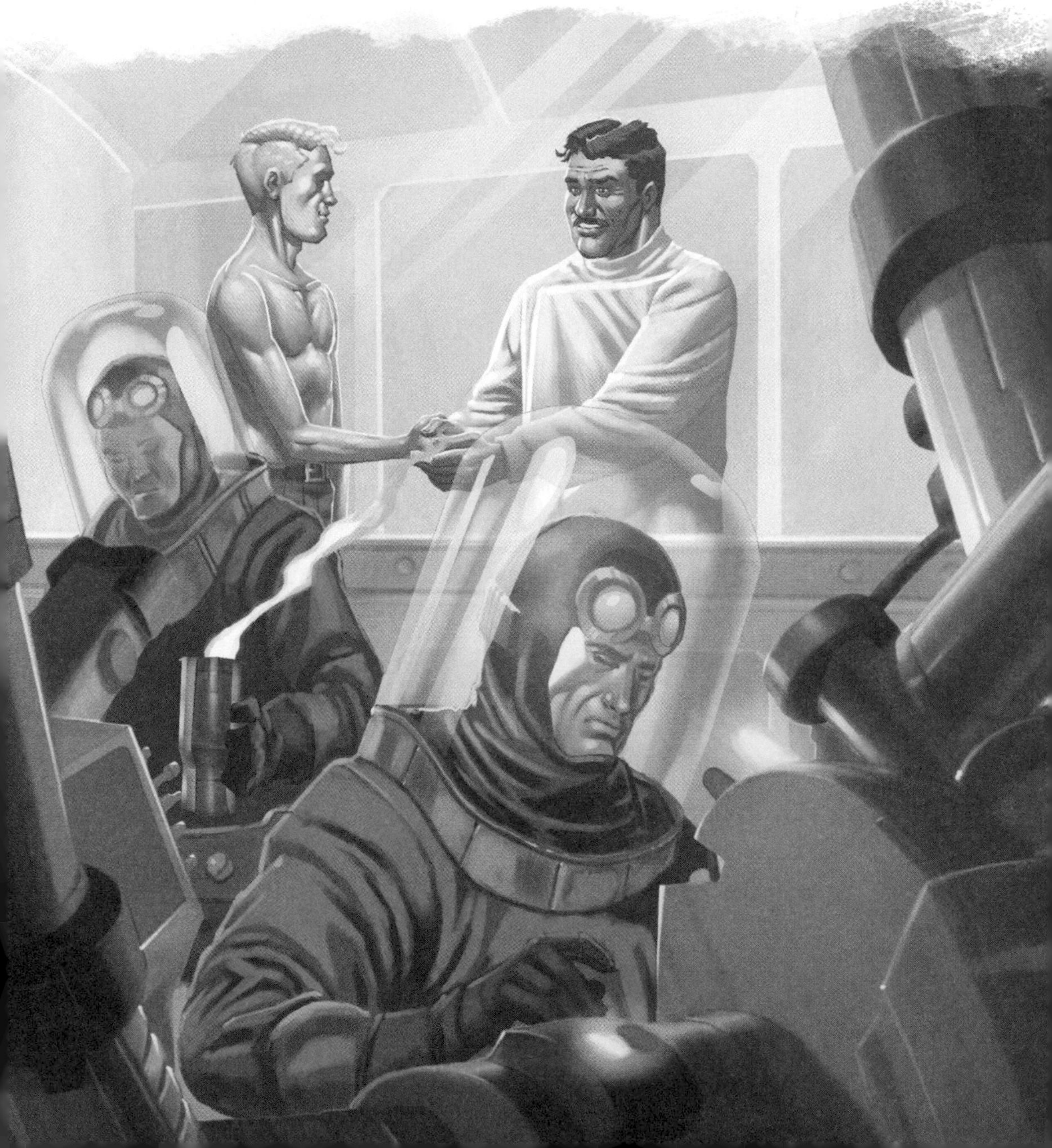

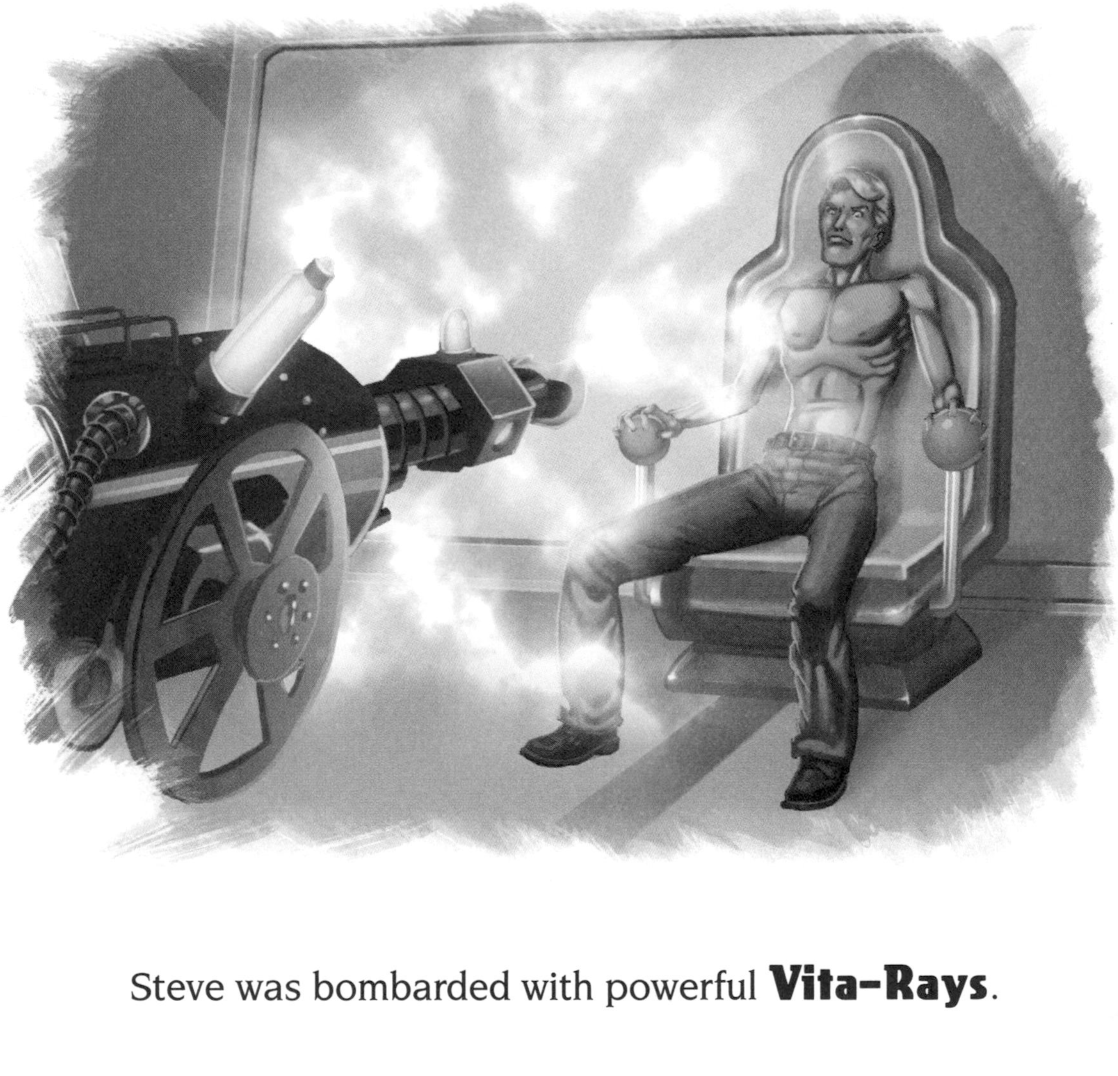

Steve was bombarded with powerful **Vita-Rays**.

The rays gave him fantastic **strength** and **speed**—more than anybody had ever possessed!

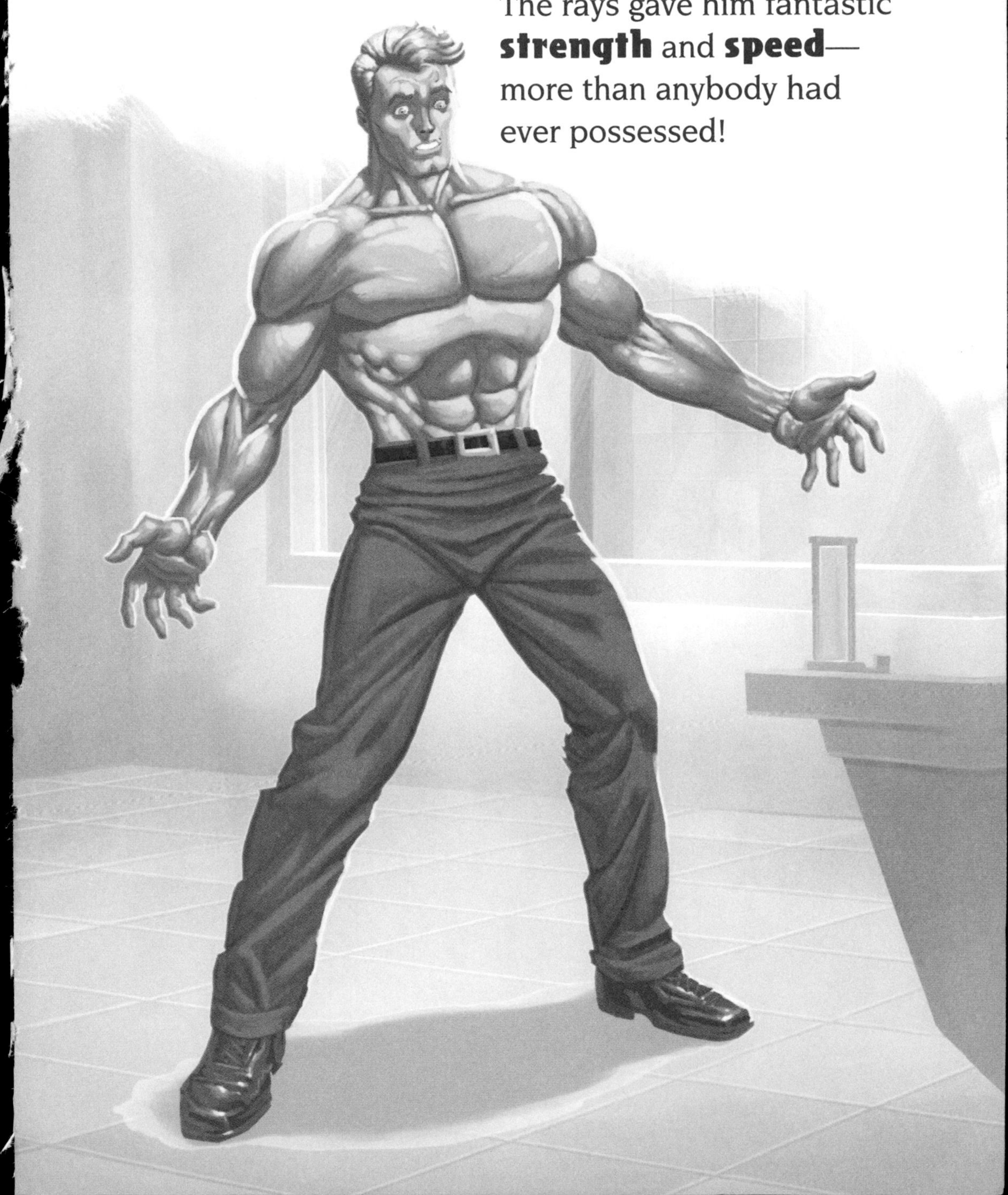

Then he trained hard so he could
defeat any foe.

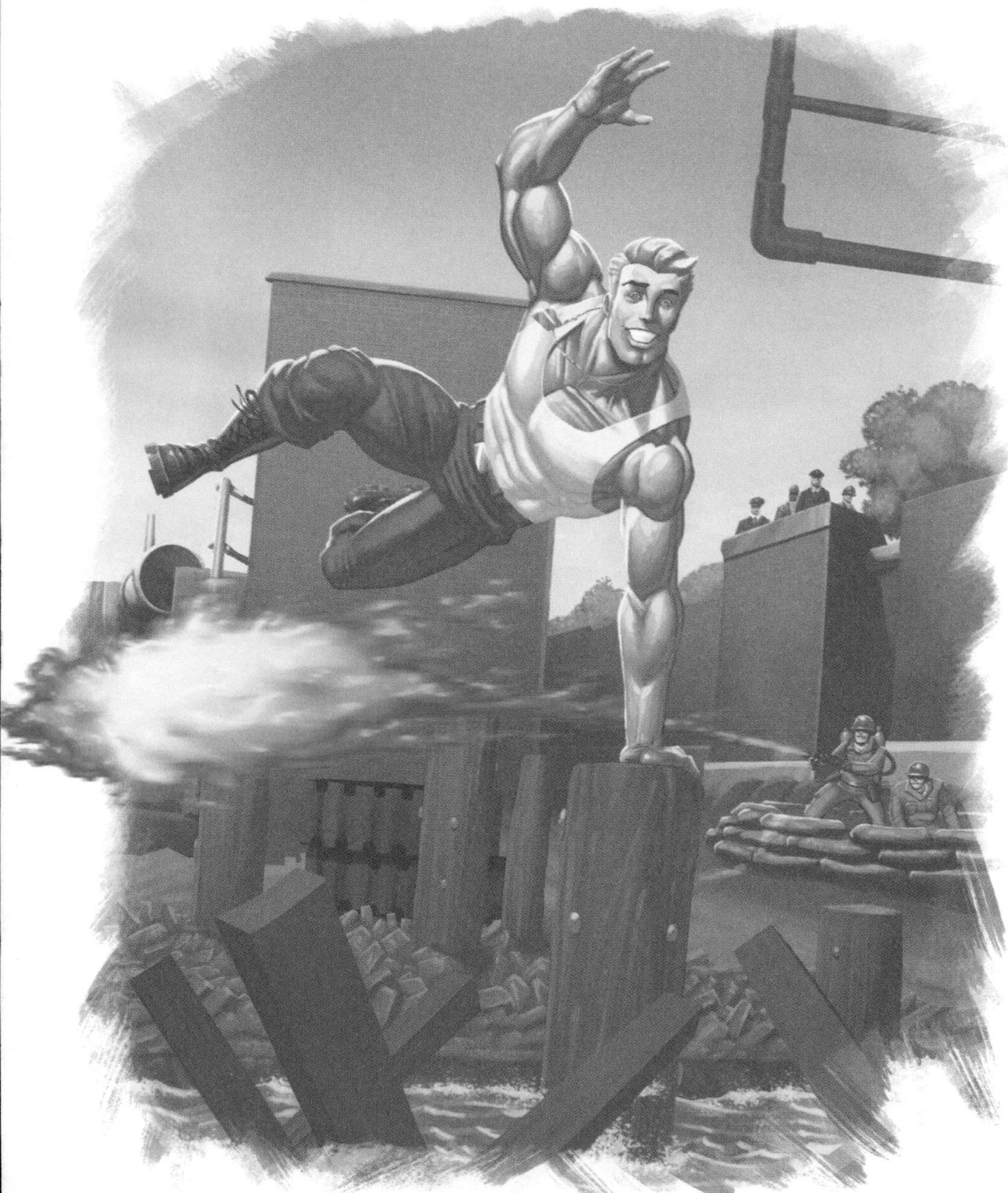

Steve used the unbreakable shield for protection.
And his red, white, and blue uniform kept his true
identity safe.

As Captain America, Steve never stopped fighting for **truth** and **freedom** . . . and he inspired good people everywhere to do the same.

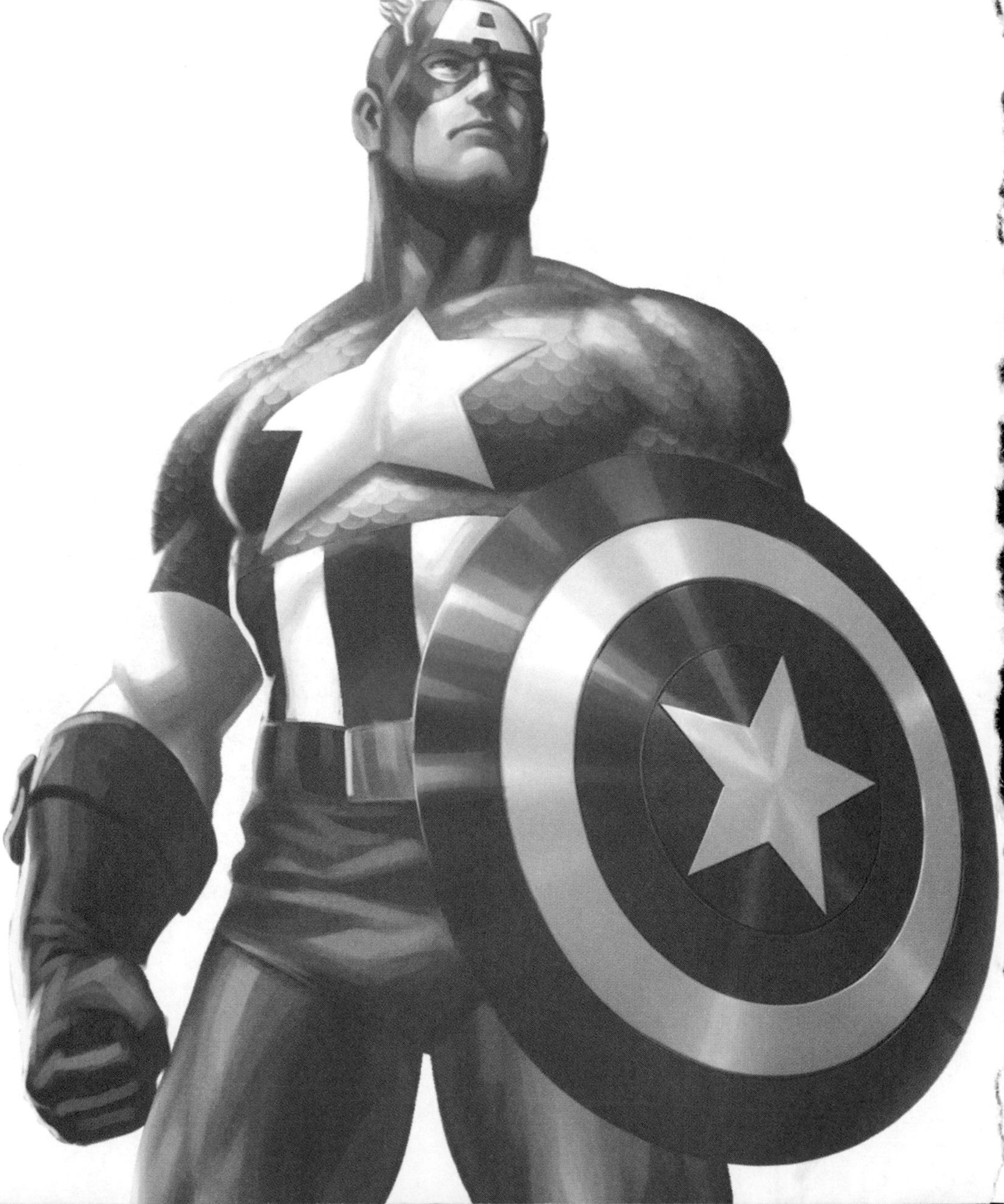